A NOTE TO PARENTS

Reading is one of the most important gifts we can give our children. How can you help your child to become interested in reading? By reading aloud!

My First Games Readers make excellent read-alouds and are the very first books your child will be able to read by him/herself. Based on the games children know and love, the goals of these books include helping your child:

- **learn sight words**
- **understand that print corresponds to speech**
- **understand that words are read from left to right and top to bottom**

Here are some tips on how to read together and how to enjoy the fun activities in the back of these books:

Reading Together

- Set aside a special time each day to read to your child. Encourage your child to comment on the story or pictures or predict what might happen next.
- After reading the book, you might wish to start lists of words that begin with a specific letter (such as the first letter of your child's name) or words your child would like to learn.
- Ask your child to read these books on his/her own. Have your child read to you while you are preparing dinner or driving to the grocery store.

Reading Activities

- The activities listed in the back of this book are designed to use and expand what children know through reading and writing. You may choose to do one activity a night, following each reading of the book.
- Keep the activities gamelike and don't forget to praise your child's efforts!

Whatever you do, have fun with this book as you pass along the joy of reading to your child. It's a gift that will last a lifetime!

Wiley Blevins, Reading Specialist
Ed.M. Harvard University

ISBN 0-439-23563-4

12 11 10 9 8 7 6 5 4 3 2 1   0 1 2 3 4 5 6/0

Illustrated by Joe Kulka
Designed by Peter Koblish

Printed in the U.S.A.
First Scholastic printing, December 2000

CANDY LAND®
Happy Birthday, Princess Lolly!

by **Jackie Glassman**
Illustrated by **Joe Kulka**

SCHOLASTIC INC.

New York   Toronto   London   Auckland   Sydney   Mexico City   New Delhi   Hong Kong

Princess Lolly is having a birthday

We are making an ice cream surprise. What do we need?

We need one bowl.

What else do we need?

The cake reads "Happy Birthday Princess Lolly!"

The bottle is labeled "Chocolate Syrup"

We need two scoops of ice cream

What else do we need?

We need three candy canes.

What else do we need?

We need four big gumdrops.

What else do we need?

We need five nuts.

What else do we need?

We need six spoonfuls of sprinkles

What else do we need?

We need seven drops of chocolate

What else do we need?

We need eight lollipops.

What else do we need?

We need Princess Lolly.

Happy Birthday, Princess Lolly!

Number Match

The Candy Land friends used a lot of food to make Princess Lolly's surprise. Can you remember how many gumdrops, lollipops, scoops of ice cream, and nuts they used? Look at the foods listed in column A. Then look at the numbers listed in column B. Now match each food in column A to a number in column B.

5

4

8

2

Create a Treat

Here is a picture of Princess Lolly's ice cream surprise. What kind of ice cream surprise would you like on your birthday? On a separate piece of paper, draw your ice cream surprise. You can also label each ingredient.

Thank-You Card

Pretend you are Princess Lolly. On a piece of paper, write a thank-you note to one of your Candy Land friends for making you the ice cream surprise. Draw a picture, too! Here is an example to help you begin.

From the Desk of Princess Lolly...

Dear Grandma Nut,

Thank you so much for the yummy ice cream surprise.

This was the best birthday ever!

The nuts were my favorite part.

I love you,
Princess Lolly

Mix-n-Match

In the story, each Candy Land friend added one new ingredient. Do you remember who added what? Match each friend to a goody.

S Is For . . .

Look at the pictures below. Which ones begin with the letter S?

A Look of Surprise

Here is a picture of Princess Lolly when her friends gave her the ice cream surprise. Tell how you think she is feeling. How would you feel if you were Princess Lolly?

Count Off

How many different kinds of food did the Candy Land friends use to make the ice cream surprise? Each new food counts as one. Look at the picture below, and add them up!

Birthday Candles

Princess Lolly is six years old today.
Below is a picture of her birthday cake.
Draw or trace the cake onto another
piece of paper. Then add the birthday
candles. How many will you draw? Why?

Answers

Number Match

5

4

8

2

S Is For . . .
These begin with *S*:

Count Off
There are seven ingredients in the ice cream surprise.

Birthday Candles
Princess Lolly's cake needs six candles. Or seven candles, if one is for good luck.

Mix-n-Match